**For Belinda, Bob, Anne,
and everyone fighting to protect
these animals in their habitat**

*A percentage of the royalties
from this book is being donated to the
Wildlife Protection Society of India.*

Copyright © 1999 by Flora McDonnell

First U.S. edition 1999

Library of Congress Cataloging-in-Publication Data
McDonnell, Flora.
Splash! / Flora McDonnell.—1st U.S. ed.
p.   cm
Summary: When the jungle animals are hot,
a baby elephant has a good solution involving the
squirting and splashing of water at the water hole.
ISBN 0-7636-0481-X
[1. Elephants—Fiction.
2. Jungle animals—Fiction.]   I. Title.
PZ7.M15437Sp   1999
[E]—dc21   98-12384

2 4 6 8 10 9 7 5 3 1

Printed in Hong Kong

This book was typeset in New Baskerville.
The pictures were done in gouache, acrylic, and watercolor.

Candlewick Press
2067 Massachusetts Avenue
Cambridge, Massachusetts 02140

Splash!

Flora McDonnell

CANDLEWICK PRESS
CAMBRIDGE, MASSACHUSETTS

Hot, hot, hot!
The elephants
are hot.

Tiger is hot.

Rhinoceros is hot.

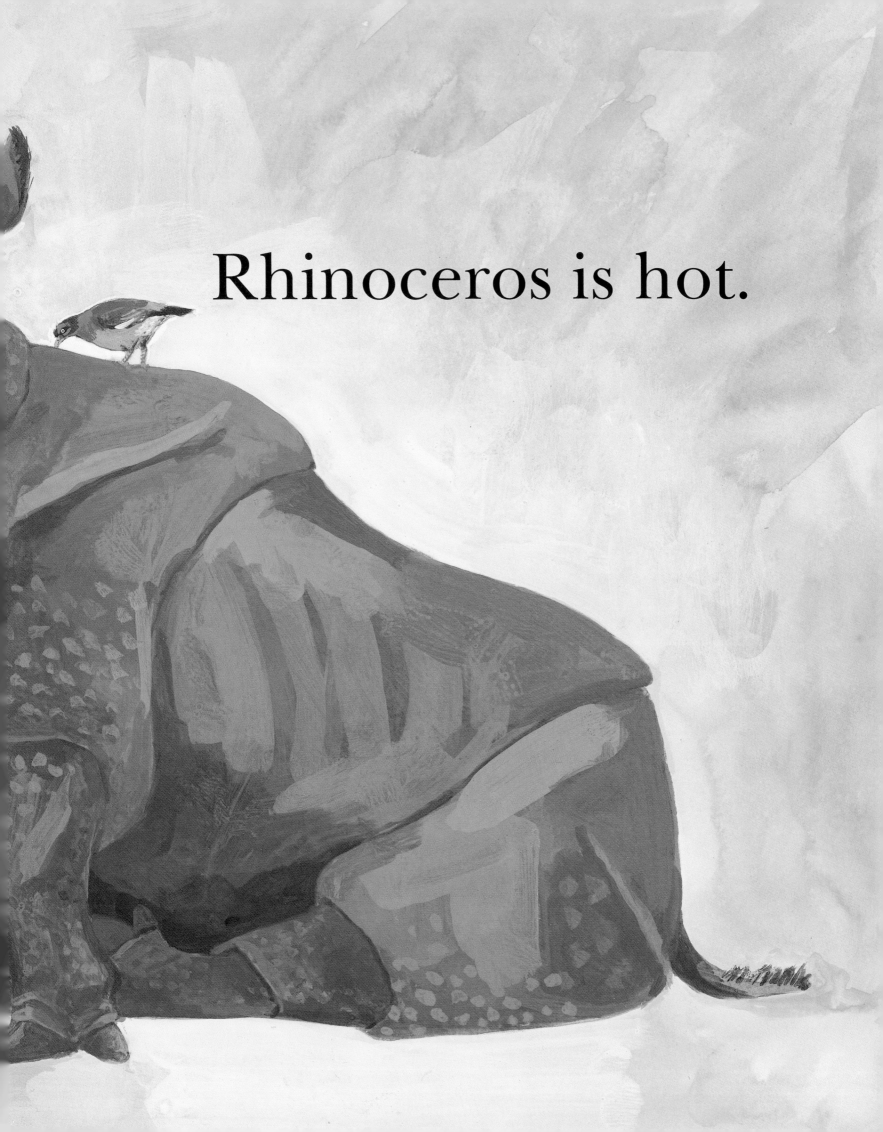

Let's follow
the baby
down to
the . . .

water.
Lovely water.

Water
to drink.
Water to . . .

squirt,
squirt,
squirt!

Splash!
goes Mother Elephant.

Splosh!

goes Rhinoceros.

Whoosh!
Sploosh!
goes Tiger.

Now Tiger is cool and happy.

Now Rhinoceros is cool and happy.

Now
Mother
Elephant
is cool
and
happy.

What
a happy,
cool,
clever
little baby
elephant!